Book text, illustrations and design by John Clarke

ISBN: 9798411723564
(paperback)

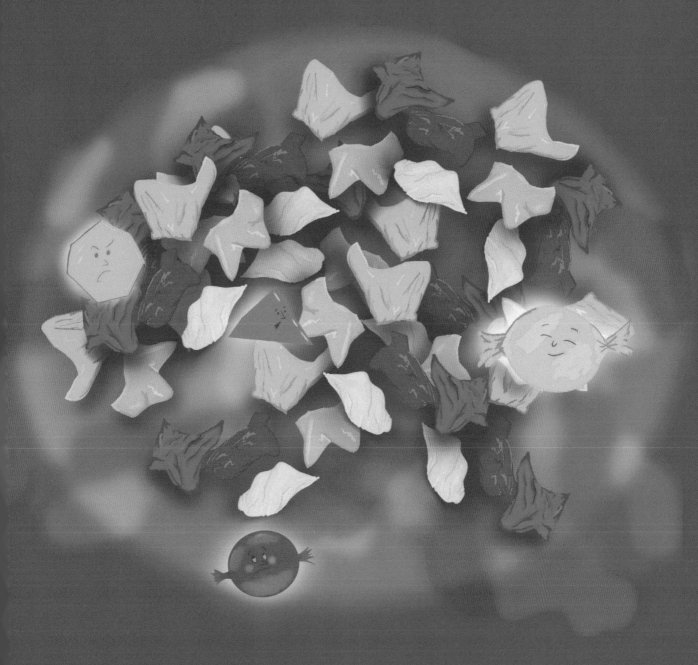

# This book
## belongs to:

_____

One Christmas morning
not so long ago,
the doorstep and windows
were covered with snow.
The carpet was smothered
with paper and bows
and the scents from the kitchen
delighted each nose.

The chocolates were opened,
every size, every flavour.
The favourites were chosen,
to nibble and savour.
The tub was passed round
and everyone munched...

On toffees and fudges and
marshmallow crunch,

on butterscotch candy
and hazelnut swirls,

pralines and coconut
and dark chocolate curls.

Silky smooth caramels
were guzzled and scoffed

as truffles and nougat
were demolished and quaffed!

With liquorice devoured
and the marzipans gone,
there were very few left
to be feasted upon.

But left down below
buried deep in the box
lay two sad and lonely,
unwanted chocs.
Unsure what had happened
or where their friends were.
They nervously waited,
trying not to despair.

*Chocolates*

One was bright red like a new holly berry.
Oh how he glistened, so shiny and merry.
On the opposite side, lay a tangerine cream.
He dozed in the darkness and he started to dream.
His wrapper, it shimmered. What a sight to admire!
It glimmered and glittered, like a warm winter fire.

They lay there and waited
as the hands swooped on by,
"Soon we'll be chosen
to go up to the sky.

Oh the things we will see
and the things we will learn.
It has to be soon.
It is surely our turn."

# The hours ticked by

and the day was soon done,
but still they were waiting
as the night time wore on.

When the lights were switched off
and the family all slept,
the chocolates took action
and slowly they crept.
They pushed past the wrappers,
their friends had been wearing
and they rose to the top
all courageous and daring.
Braced for the battle,
they'd escape from the tin,
go over the top
and the fun would begin.

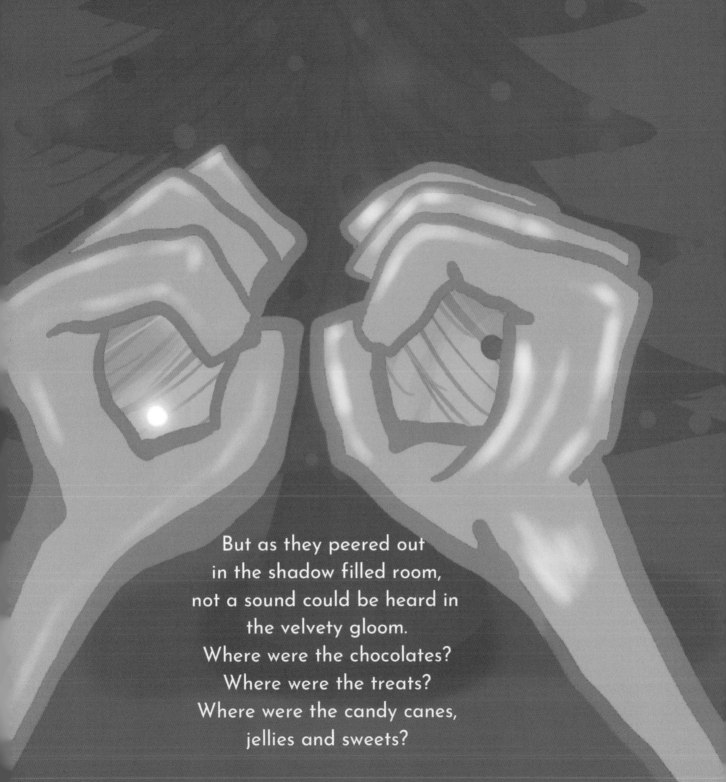

But as they peered out
in the shadow filled room,
not a sound could be heard in
the velvety gloom.
Where were the chocolates?
Where were the treats?
Where were the candy canes,
jellies and sweets?

"Where have they gone?"
The orange cream hissed,
"I don't know," was the answer
"There's something we've missed."
Sat on the edge
they gazed all around,
dropped down their rope
and slid to the ground.

Chocola

The chocolates had vanished.
Oh where could they be?
Had our chocs now uncovered
**A great mystery?**

They scurried about
under tables and sofas,
clambered up slippers
and wandered round loafers.
They searched high and low
but all with no luck.
They searched every cranny.
They searched every nook.

They wandered the rooms
and the hallways that night.
Wherever they looked
not a choc was in sight.
Tired and aching,
they lay down to think
and huddled together
by the cold kitchen sink.

When out of a corner
a whisker was spied.
Then a nose and some ears
and two twinkling eyes.
It scampered towards them
And said with a grin,
"What are you doing?
Are you out of your tin!?"

"You're going to be eaten!
Quick go and hide!
If they find you you'll end up
in someone's inside."

""No, no," said the strawberry,
"That surely can't be.
We've sat there for hours now
under that tree.
Nobody's eaten us.
Nobody's tried.
How can we end up
inside their insides?"

But the mouse simply chuckled
and then he was gone.
So the chocolates continued
the quest they were on.

They sifted the flour
and grilled the smoked bacon,
to find out exactly
where the others were taken.

Like detectives they quizzed
all the food that they found
but no one could tell them
the word on the ground.

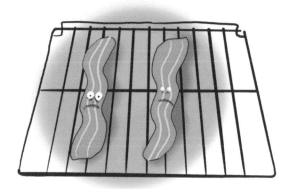

The packets were sealed.

The eggs wouldn't crack.

The tins in the cupboard
simply showed them their back.

The peach made no speech and the milk wouldn't spill...

There was nothing more for it
They were doomed... until....

When all hope was lost
and the morning grew near,
our chocs' lonely mission
was suddenly clear.
They stumbled across
a most marvellous book,
"Chocolate: the answers"
they must take a look.

With heaving and pushing,
they knocked the book down.
Lifted the cover,
turned it around,
hoisting the pages,
they read and they read
and quickly those chocolates
were filled up with dread.
The horrors they found
and the nightmares they saw;
soufflés and puddings
and pastries galore!

Chocolate:
the answers

Smothered in chocolate
with chocolatey fillings,
with sauces and centres
all **ooZing** and **Spilling**

Melted hot chocolate
and chocolate ganache...
It was enough to bring anyone
out in a rash!

Right there they decided
it wasn't too late.
These two would not share
their friend's terrible fate.
They raced through the kitchen
and searched til they found
a hole in the wall, low down
near the ground.

Inside it they crept,
whilst feeling quite certain
they'd never be found
in the dining room skirting.

They dusted and cleaned.
They polished and swept,
'til tired and exhausted
they finally slept.
Time soon wore on and
their home it took shape,
with blankets and cushions
carpets and drapes.

They lived there quite cosy
in their newly made house,
Tangerine, Strawberry and
their neighbour; the mouse.

Now I've heard it said
that each year they will creep
to the hole in the skirting
and carefully peep
to seek out the chocolates
who are left in the tin;
they find them and save them

and welcome them in.
So next time you wonder,
who's eaten your chocs,
be sure that they haven't
crept out of the box!

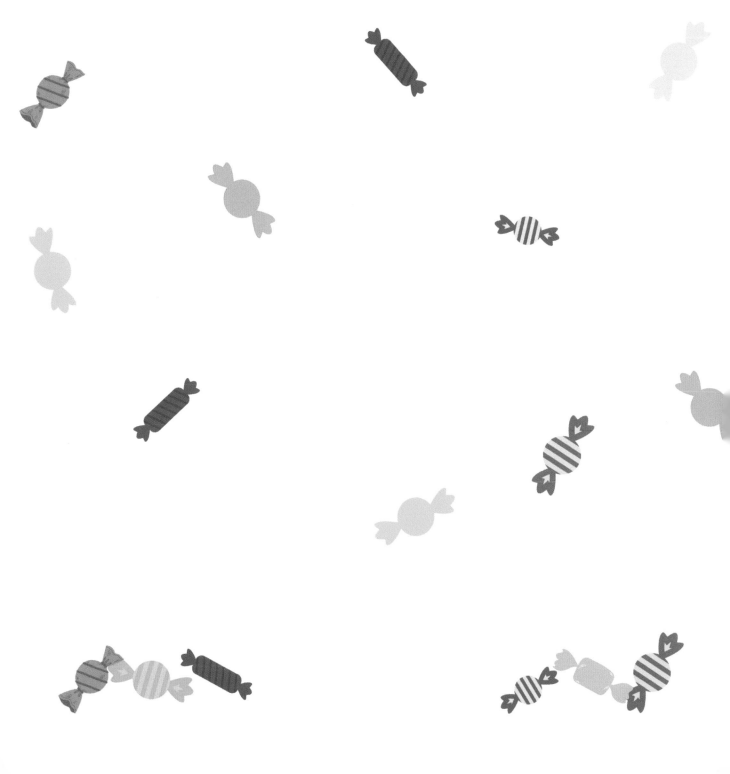

Printed in Great Britain
by Amazon